I0712687

Melissa By The Sea

Written and Illustrated by
Taurean Nelson

This book is dedicated to anyone with a dream, anything can happen as long as you believe...

Here's a tale about Melissa
a girl oh so bright.
She had an idea to sell,
sparklers by the beach at night

Pitched the idea to friends
but they didn't seem to agree

2

It made Melissa sad BUT she just had to see.....

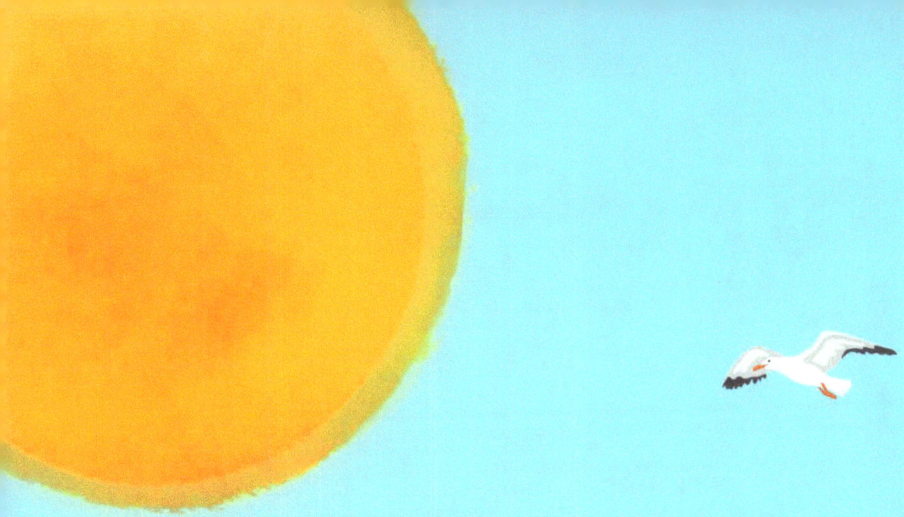

So she bought the Sparklers
built the stands
stood by the beach

THEN

I wonder what's gonna happen next?

Yea, me too

Yea, me too

JINX!!

5

Children lined up,
an oh so wonderful thing

Melissa sold out that day,
right on the beach

learning a lesson

And of course, almost everything is better with friends

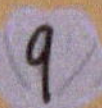

But sometimes they wont see

Its dark in here
zzzz
Is this really necessary?

So even if you're
all alone
gulp

Be all you can be!

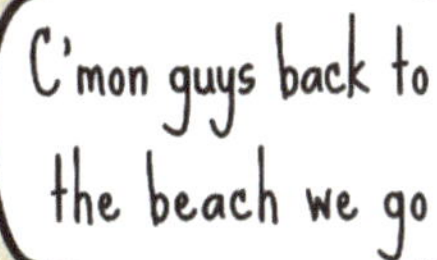

12

THE END

See Ya!

Bye

Bye